The NUTCRACKER

Jane Ray

Christmas Eve is the most magical night of the year, when the house is scented with wood smoke and spices, and there are secrets under every bed! Snow whispers down like feathers and children wait, breathless, for the curtain to rise on Christmas Day . . .

For my wonderful Clara

J.R.

ORCHARD BOOKS

First published in Great Britain in 2015 by The Watts Publishing Group
This edition published in 2016

2 4 6 8 10 9 7 5 3

Text and illustrations © Jane Ray, 2015

A CIP catalogue record for this book is available from the British Library.

ISBN 978 1 40833 644 1

Printed and bound in China

Orchard Books
An imprint of Hachette Children's Group
Part of The Watts Publishing Group Limited
Carmelite House
50 Victoria Embankment
London EC4Y 0DZ

An Hachette UK Company
www.hachette.co.uk

www.hachettechildrens.co.uk

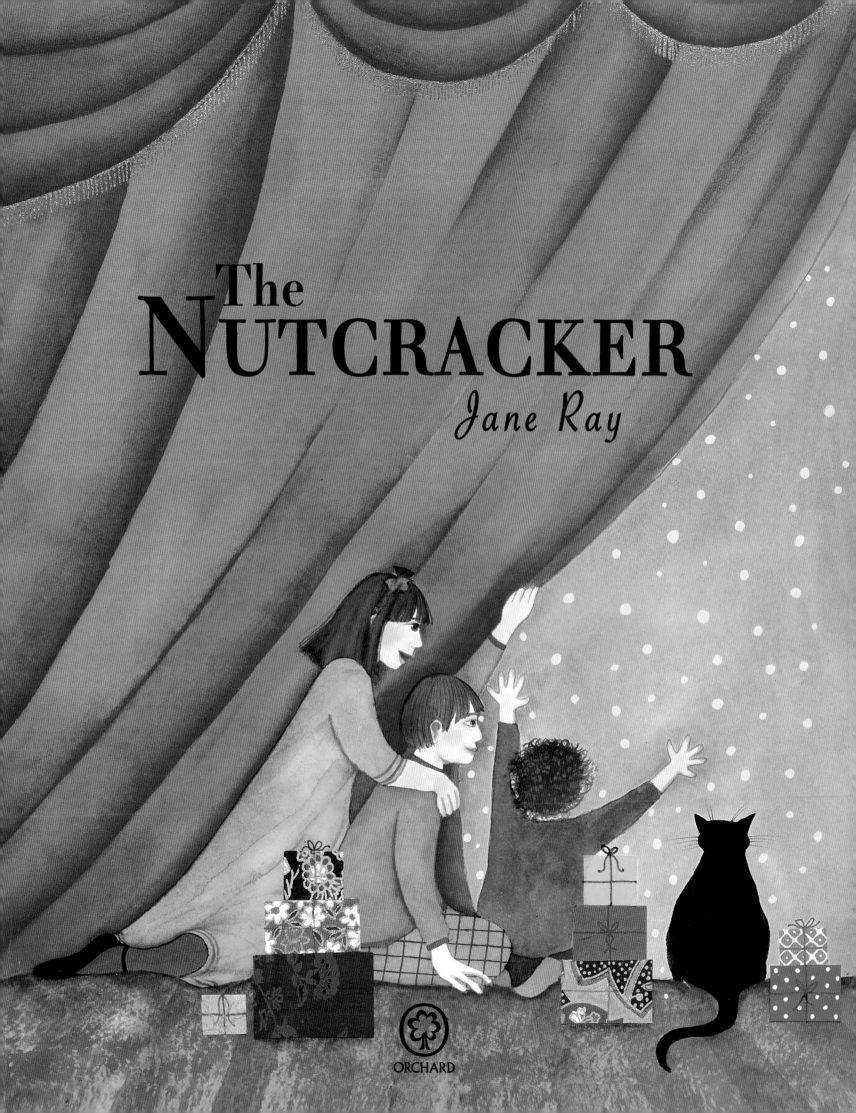

The NUTCRACKER

Jane Ray

ORCHARD

THE FRONT DOOR was flung wide to welcome guests to the Ernst family Christmas party. Friends and relatives, young and old, all came, stamping the snow off their boots and greeting each other with hugs and laughter.

Clara, Freddie and George, dressed in their best clothes, hopped up and down with excitement.

The guests gathered around the huge Christmas tree.

It flickered with candlelight, its branches hung with sugared

almonds, gingerbread and delicate glass ornaments.

Under its fragrant boughs, the presents were piled up.

The children scampered around it like

excited puppies.

But Clara was looking out for her godfather,
Herr Drosselmeyr, whom the children all loved.
There was no guest as interesting as him because he
brought the most wonderful gifts imaginable!

Herr Drosselmeyr was a toymaker, an inventor, a magician. His back was bowed and he wore a patch over one eye. But the other eye was a bright and piercing blue and sparkled with mischief.

And there he was at last, wrapped in a cloak the colour of midnight.

From its velvety folds he produced his gifts . . .

For Freddie, a troupe of soldiers, complete with cannon and muskets. For little George, a wooden horse on wheels, and a tin trumpet.

And for Clara?

Her godfather handed her
a large box. With trembling
hands, Clara lifted the lid
and pulled back the
tissue paper.

Inside was the strangest doll she had ever seen. He was made of painted wood, and had a red coat and pink cheeks. But most odd of all was his mouth, which was wide and filled with little wooden teeth.

Herr Drosselmeyr put a hazelnut between the doll's teeth and lifted its arms. The nutshell cracked open and a sweet kernel fell into Clara's hand. She was enchanted and flung her arms around her godfather. How like him to make her something so unusual!

Freddie suddenly grabbed the Nutcracker from Clara's hands.

"He wants to join my soldiers," he said. But as he ducked away through the guests, the Nutcracker clattered to the floor and skittered across the polished boards, breaking one little wooden arm.

Freddie was marched from the room. Clara was inconsolable.

Herr Drosselmeyr picked up the wounded Nutcracker and carefully put him back in his box. "We'll leave him under the Christmas tree for now," he said, wiping Clara's tears, "and tomorrow I'll glue him back together."

Then the grandfather clock in the hall struck eight and dinner
was served – roasted meats, plum pudding and fruit jellies!

Everyone felt happy to be among friends. When dinner was over,
the candles on the Christmas tree flickered out one by one, the
fire began to die down, and the sleepy children were sent to bed.

Clara was woken by the clock in the hall striking midnight. Immediately, she remembered her Nutcracker doll, still in his box under the tree. He must be cold and lonely in the dark. She slipped out of bed and crept downstairs.

The house was shadowy in the moonlight. The candles were all snuffed out and the fire had burnt down to a heap of glowing embers. The only sounds were the ticking of the grandfather clock, and an owl calling from the snowy garden.

In a dark corner by the tree, Clara could just make out tiny lights glowing.

Puzzled, she looked closer – and then gasped when she realised that she was looking at dozens of pairs of beady eyes, peeping through the gloom. They belonged to an army of mice – huge mice, growing before her eyes, until they were bigger than rats, bigger than cats, even, and growing still more!

With a great rustling and creaking, the Christmas tree seemed to grow bigger, until the whole room became a snowy forest.

The mice, led by their fearsome Mouse King, began to advance, their eyes glowing like the dying embers of the fire. They surrounded the Christmas tree, intent on stealing the presents piled under its branches. But then came a rallying call from George's tin trumpet, and Freddie's toy soldiers rose up as one. The little wooden horse rolled forward, hauling the cannon into place, and the soldiers set to, loading it with sugared almonds.

Together they advanced on the mouse army, with muskets and rattling sabres.

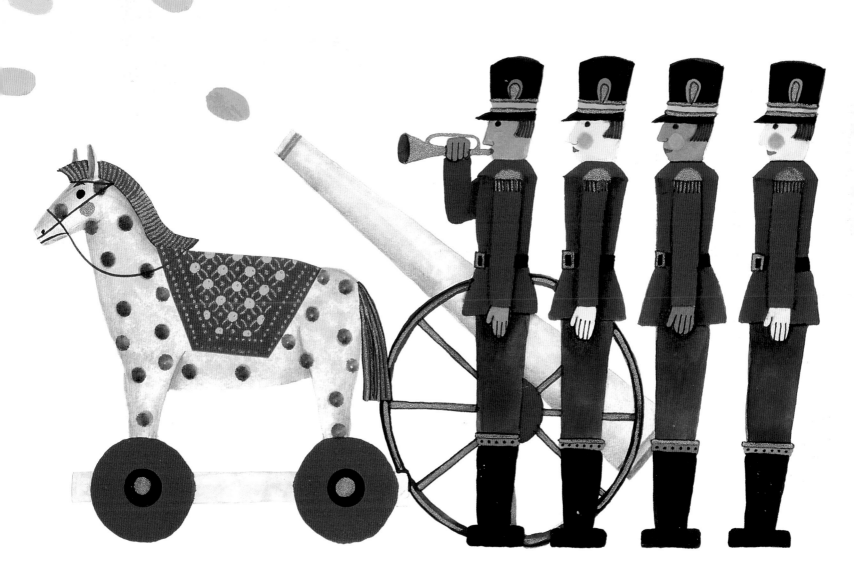

Suddenly, to Clara's astonishment, the Nutcracker was by her side, no longer a strange little wooden doll but instead a fine young man. This Nutcracker drew his sword and challenged the Mouse King!

They fought fiercely, swords clashing. Clara seized a candy cane and charged at the mice. Smoke plumed from the cannon as the opposing armies battled across the snowy carpet.

The Nutcracker was brave, but Clara could see that with his cracked arm he was beginning to lose the fight.

She knew she had to act, or the Mouse King would triumph and there would be no Christmas presents in the morning.

She took off her slipper and flung it as hard as she could. It hit the Mouse King squarely, right between the eyes. Seeing their leader grounded, the mice lost heart. They ran to their king, grabbed him by the tail, and pulling him behind them, they fled through the trees, vanquished!

The Nutcracker turned to Clara. "You saved my life," he said.

"Let me bandage your arm," said Clara. She took her shawl and wrapped it firmly.

Recovering his breath, the Nutcracker said, "To thank you, I am going to take you on a magical journey."

He took her hand and led her through trees heavy with snow and sparkling with frost, but Clara felt no cold, just bubbling excitement. They came to a lake where a boat with silken sails lay at anchor. They crossed the water, sailing into great white clouds edged with pink like candy floss.

The rocking of the boat
made Clara sleepy and
she began to drift
and dream . . .

She awoke as the boat anchored by a beautiful winter garden. The trees were made of striped candy, sprinkled with icing sugar and hung with bright little sweets. Crystalised flowers scattered the sugary lawn. It was like walking across a wedding cake!

"Where are we?" asked Clara, aghast.

"This is my kingdom," the Nutcracker said.

There was a delicate tinkling sound and the Sugar Plum Fairy

appeared before them.

"Welcome to the Kingdom of Sweets," she said.

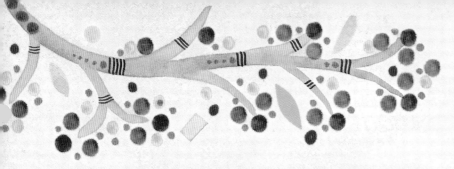

Clara and the Nutcracker were seated before a curtained
stage, and given cups of hot chocolate to warm them.
The Sugar Plum Fairy clicked her fingers, and Clara and the
Nutcracker watched spellbound as music filled the air.

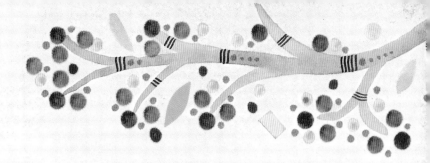

The curtains parted and the sweets of every land danced before them.
There was marshmallow from Russia, delicate rose-scented Turkish
Delight, and then Madam BonBon from France arrived, with all
her sweet little gingerbread children clustering under her skirts.

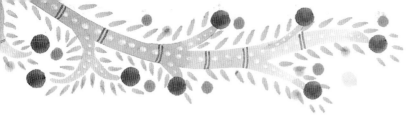

A large china tea cup was trundled onto the stage next,

and a troupe of Chinese acrobats leapt out of it,

juggling mooncakes and fortune cookies.

Close on the acrobats' heels were Spanish dancers with baskets of
rich, dark chocolate and marzipan. Clara clapped her hands
with delight, enchanted by everything she saw.

The last dance of all was that of the Sugar Plum Fairy
herself, accompanied by sugar snowflakes
and crystalised flowers. She held out
her hand to Clara and the Nutcracker,
inviting them to join her.

Round and round they circled, as the music soared

and the sky grew pink with the rising sun.

Clara's head began to whirl and she felt

she was floating with happiness . . .

. . . and the next thing she knew, Freddie and George were

jumping on her bed. "Wake up, Clara," they said, laughing.

"Christmas has come!"

Clara sat up and looked around her, astonished.

Had it all been a dream?

But why were there sugar flowers in her hair?

And how was the Nutcracker a doll again, there by

her side, his broken arm completely mended?

There was no time for questions. Freddie and George were

impatient to start unwrapping the presents under the tree.

IT WAS CHRISTMAS MORNING AT LAST!